It Zwibble
and the Big Birthday Party

Written by Lisa Werenko

Illustrated by Tom Ross

SCHOLASTIC INC.

New York   Toronto   London   Auckland   Sydney

Dedicated to our moms and dads,
brothers and sisters.

ISBN 0-590-43861-1

12 11 10 9 8 7 6 5 4 3 2 1   0 1 2 3/9

Printed in the U.S.A.

One day in the Buzzville Forest, It Zwibble (the dinosaur fairy) and the little Zwibble Dibbles were making leaf boats for the frogs in the frog pond.

"How old is the earth?" asked little Dipper.

"Oh, billions of years old," said the fairy.

"Has it ever had a birthday party?" asked another.

"Gee, I don't know," said It Zwibble. "We can check the fairy legend book. It's full of all sorts of information."

They hurried home to the Zwibble Dibble Mill. "It does have a birthday!" said the fairy. "It says here that the earth's birthday is on the first full moon of May. They call it the Flower Moon."

"Imagine how sad you would feel if you were billions of years old and no one had ever given you a birthday party," said It Zwibble. It Zwibble decided not to let another year go by. "The Earth's birthday is only one week away. Let's throw it the best birthday party ever! We'll invite all the children. It wouldn't be much of a party without them!"

The forest friends thought It Zwibble had a great idea.
All but Craighead the Shrew. "Who ever heard of a birthday
party for the earth?" he said. "Ridiculous!"

"Don't be a party pooper!" said Tu the Toucan. "It will be
a lot of fun."

It Zwibble wrote invitations while he tried to think of the best birthday gift for the earth. Many invitations later, he still had not come up with an idea. "Beesweeney", he said. "I want the gift to be special. The earth gives us so many gifts all year — the mountains, the oceans, the rivers, the trees, the flowers...."

All of a sudden, It Zwibble jumped.
"I've got it!" he cried. He hurried downstairs.

"I've got the best idea for the earth's surprise gift! I better get started right away!" The forest animals had never seen the fairy so excited.

"It must be a humdinger of an idea," said Fred the Moose. While It Zwibble worked on the gift, everybody else got busy with the party preparations.

The Zwibble Dibble Mill was bustling.

Cobb the Beaver took out his secret family recipe for the BEAVERBLUPERSUPERDUPERBIRTHDAYPARTYSURPRISE CAKE. Cobb let the Zwibble Dibbles add all the surprises — popcorn, bubble gum, and chocolate syrup. Orbit wanted to add beans and baloney.

Tu the Toucan pulled tools out of the pockets in his little feather coat and whipped up a wonderful bandstand and dance floor. "Just what every great party needs," said Tu, "a place to boogie." The Zwibble Dibbles helped to paint it in bold bright colors.

Fred the Moose made flower baskets for the tables. The Zwibble Dibbles helped. "Those buttercups sure make it special," said Fred.

The forest animals sang while they wrapped all the party favors for the children. The Zwibble Dibbles had fun planning all the games.

Finally everything was ready. The Zwibble Dibble Mill had never looked so great. Everybody wondered what the Big Birthday Gift could be. It Zwibble said, "It's a surprise. We'll have to wait and open it with the children!"

"This party is going to be a blast!" said the toucan.

"Oh, maybe I will come," said the shrew.

"The guests will be arriving soon," said the fairy. They all got spruced up. Tu the Toucan fluffed his feather coat. Even Craighead picked out a snazzy bow tie! The Zwibble Dibbles could hardly wait to meet all the children.

Five o'clock, six o'clock, seven o'clock, eight. They waited. But nobody came.

"Where is everyone?" asked little Dipper.

"See, I told you this was a dumb idea!" said the shrew. "Nobody cares about the earth."

At the Zwibble Dibble Mill, no one felt much like celebrating anymore. "What's the use of having a party when the guests don't even show up?" said Tu. They all went to bed without saying another word.

The dinosaur fairy stayed up all alone. "I don't understand
it," he said. "I know the children love the earth as much as
we do. And the party was such a great idea. Maybe they
didn't like the invitation?" Then the fairy remembered
something he had forgotten to do. "Beesweeney!
I really goofed," he said. "I got so excited about the gift that
I forgot to mail the invitations!"

In a few more hours the earth's birthday would be over. It Zwibble looked up to the stars. "I wish there was some way I could save the earth's birthday!" Suddenly he got an idea.

It Zwibble gathered up
a bag of stardust.

Then he said some magic words.
He winked, he blinked, he made himself
shrink till he was just the size
of a small potato.

Then It Zwibble took off,
flying to the stars.

He traveled to children's homes all over the world. The children could hardly believe their eyes when It Zwibble woke them from their dreams. They had never seen a fairy before. "Why, you fit in the palm of my hand!" they said.
When It Zwibble told them about the earth's birthday party, they all wanted to come.

It Zwibble sprinkled magic stardust on them so they could fly! In no time at all they arrived at the Mill! The forest animals and Zwibble Dibbles hurried outside when they heard the children's shouts of joy. The Zwibble Dibbles shouted, "It Zwibble has saved the earth's birthday!"

Everyone laughed when they realized they were all in their pajamas. Tu the Toucan changed the sign.

At the party there was so much to do! There was singing and dancing. There were games for everybody to play. Even Craighead the Shrew had a great time.

WELCOME TO THE EARTH'S PAJAMA BIRTHDAY PARTY

When they gathered around the birthday cake, everyone made a special wish for the planet earth. Then they blew out the candles.

The time finally came to open the earth's BIG surprise gift. Everyone wanted to see what it was.

"LOOK! IT'S A MOUNTAIN OF SEEDS FOR THE MOST BEAUTIFUL FLOWERS!" they cried. "HAPPY BIRTHDAY, PLANET EARTH!"

The children unwrapped their party favors — brand-new tools to help them plant the earth's birthday gift.

The party was a HIT! The dinosaur fairy was never happier. "Let's give the earth a party every year!" he said.

The fairy took the children home by a special route,
through the path of the Milky Way. They saw how large their
universe was, how vast the starry dome. For the first time,
they looked at their beautiful earth and saw the planet,
their home.

"THE MOST BEAUTIFUL PLANET IS OUR HOME!"

When the celebration was over, the Zwibble Dibbles and
the forest animals waved good-bye to the children. "Come
back again next year!" they cried.